AuthorHouse™
1663 Liberty Drive
Bloomington, IN 47403
www.authorhouse.com
Phone: 1 (800) 839-8640

Published by AuthorHouse 03/14/2019

ISBN: 978-1-7283-0259-1 (sc)
ISBN: 978-1-7283-0260-7 (e)

Library of Congress Control Number: 2019902464

Print information available on the last page.

This book is printed on acid-free paper.

authorHOUSE®

Toby and the Best Dog Ever

Meg Patch

What a morning to wake up to! It was a beautiful sunny day when Toby decided to roll out of bed. The sun was shining and had warmed his fur nicely. He looked to the side to see his two kitties, Dennis and Paige still snoring away in the morning heat.

"I must be up early," he thought. He began his routine like every other day. He let himself out through his doggy door, stopped at his usual spots in the yard, rolled around in the freshly cut grass and then headed back inside for breakfast. Munching away on his food, Dennis and Paige finally stretched out of bed when all of a sudden, Toby saw something he'd never seen before in the house.

"Best Dog Ever...what is that? What does that mean?" Toby said nervously. "A new collar...who could that be for?"

He already had a beautiful red collar on that he loved and that his owners had picked out especially for him.

"It must be for a new dog!!", he thought. "Oh No!", and ran outside.

Dennis and Paige ran out after him.

"Toby wait, please stop. What's wrong? You left before you even finished breakfast."

"Paige, didn't you see the new collar hanging up? Our owners are going to get a new dog...The Best Dog Ever. That's what the collar said!! What am I going to do?"

Dennis felt bad for Toby and wanted desperately to help his friend.

"Toby, why don't we all go for a walk and talk about this. You will feel better once you get some energy out and get some fresh air. It's a beautiful day for a walk."

The three friends began walking and talking and wondering about the new dog that was coming.

"I wonder if it will be a big dog or a small dog. A small dog could be fun, it would be like having another cat, right Toby," Paige said with excitement.

"I don't know. It looked like a bigger collar to me, just like my size. Maybe they want another Lab. Do you think I did something wrong? I only chewed one pair of shoes and I stopped stealing socks out of the laundry baskets."

"Do you think they will get more cats?," Paige asked.

"I don't think so," said Dennis. They already have their paws full with you and all the trouble you cause."

The friends walked and explored all morning not realizing all the places they had visited. All of a sudden, Toby stopped.

"My collar!! My red collar, it must have fallen off somewhere. I don't have it on. I must have lost it. I can't go home without a collar, especially with a new dog coming to the house. Please help me look for it!"

Toby, Dennis and Paige set out in search of the red collar. They re-traced their steps and checked under rocks and leaves, through the mud and behind every tree. But no collar. By now, Toby's paws were all muddy and the three friends were tired and hungry.

They slowly walked back toward the house and Toby started to whimper and cry.

"I can't go home without my collar. We've been gone all day, what if the new dog is already there?"

Then he heard it…

"Toby… Toby, come here. We have something to show you. Time to come in Toby."

Toby looked at Dennis and Paige and slowly started walking up the sidewalk to the house. His kitties could barely watch but they followed behind him to see what was going to happen.

"Toby, look at your dirty paws! You three must have been busy today!"

Toby's owners gently cleaned his feet as they always did and gave him a rub over his back and along his face. He loved this part of the day and was happy to be home with his owners. For a moment, he forgot all about the new dog that was probably inside right now.

"Toby, what happened to your collar??," they asked.

"Oh no," he thought, I wish they didn't notice it was gone. I hope they aren't mad.

"Come on in Toby, we've got something special for you."

He slowy followed them in and was nervously looking for the new dog.

He sat next to them in the kitchen waiting for the news. He couldn't bear to look up for fear that the other dog would be starring him in the face and wearing The Best Dog Ever collar…

Then he felt something clip around his neck.

"Toby, your new collar was delivered! What do you think? Who's the Best Dog Ever! You are, that's who!", his owners exclaimed.

Toby could not believe his ears, it WAS for him! HE was the Best Dog Ever. The collar had been for him all along. He jumped with excitement and pranced all over the kitchen showing off his new gift. Toby could hear Dennis and Paige cheering for him from behind the table and he was so happy that his friends has been there to share the news with him.

"What a day!" Toby said to his kitties as he curled up onto his bed. "I still can't believe everything that happened today. And after all that, I can't believe that I am the Best Dog Ever!"

Dennis and Paige snuggled up next to Toby as they did every night for bedtime.

"We can," said Dennis with a giant yawn. "You've always been the Best Dog Ever to us."

Printed in the United States
By Bookmasters